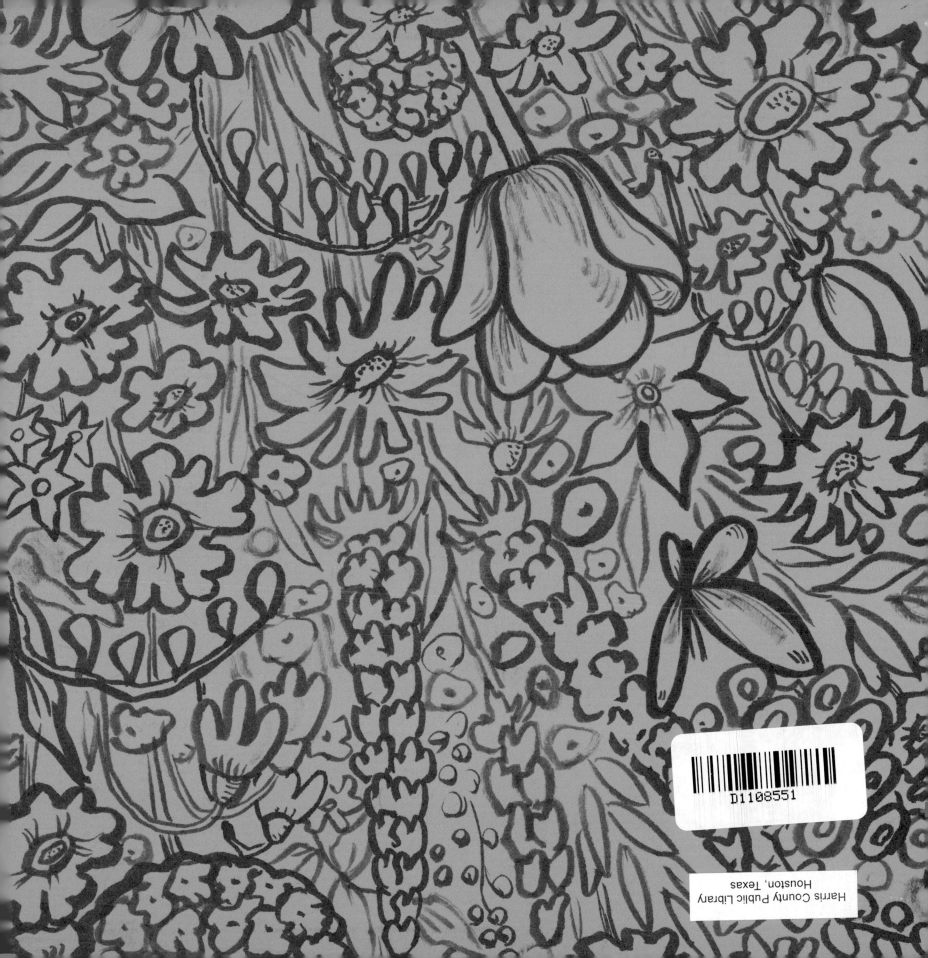

it took him a minute to realize
that he wasn't dreaming.

And when Old Bear walked out
into the beautiful spring day,

He poked his head out of his den
to see if it was still snowing.
He blinked. And blinked again.

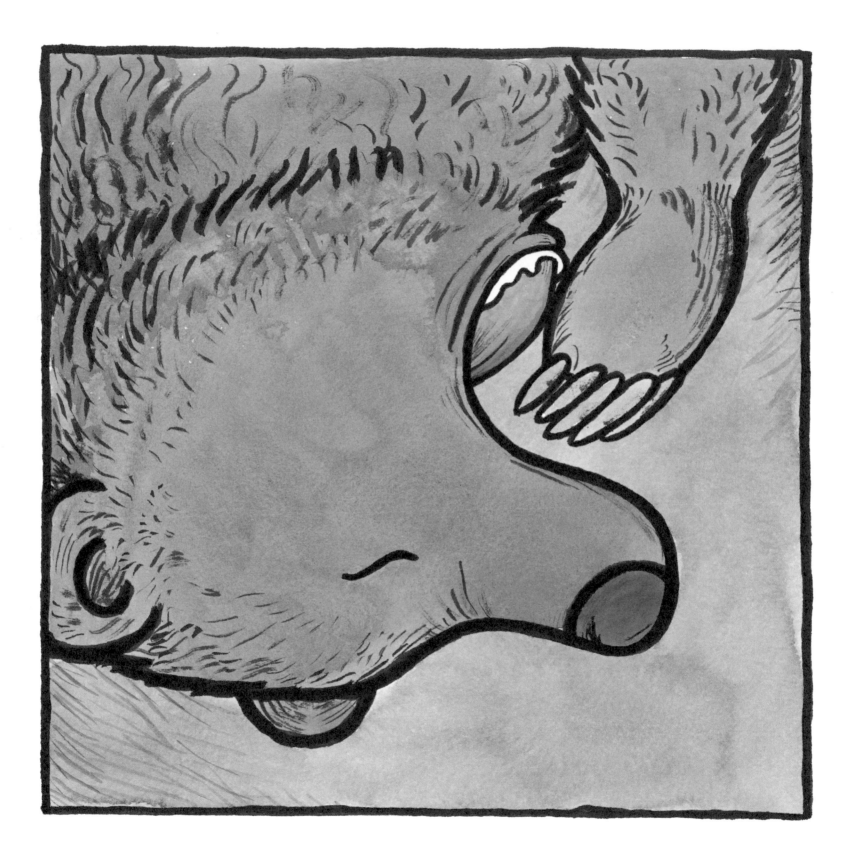

When he finally woke up,
it seemed to him that no time had passed
since he had fallen asleep.
He yawned. He stretched.

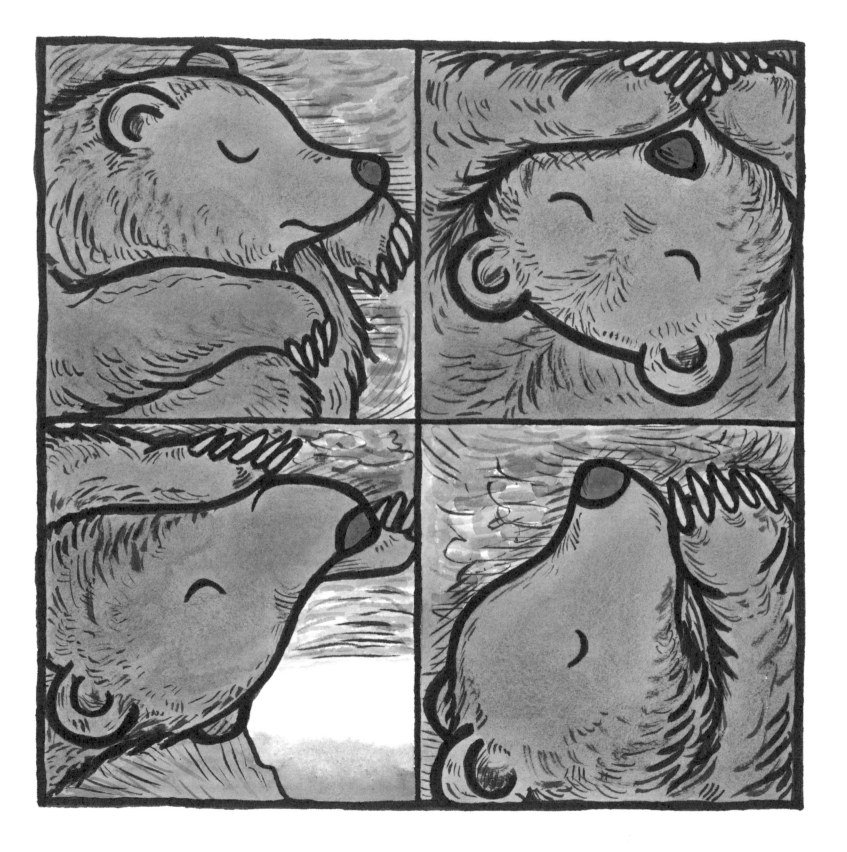

**Old Bear slept and dreamed,
dreamed and slept.**

It was night, and the sky was blazing with stars of all colors.
The cold went on forever.

After that, he dreamed that winter was back.
The world was covered in ice.

Everything was yellow and orange and brown,
even the birds and the fish and the water.

**Next, he dreamed of autumn.**

Part of the sky clouded over,
and it rained blueberries.

Then he dreamed that it was summer.
The sun was a daisy, and the leaves were butterflies.

**The flowers were as big as trees.
He took a nap in a giant pink crocus.**

He dreamed that spring had come
and he was a cub again.

Soon he was dreaming.

**B**y the time Old Bear
fell asleep for the winter,
it was snowing hard.

**For Virginia**

Old Bear. Copyright © 2008 by Kevin Henkes. All rights reserved. Manufactured in China. For information address HarperCollins Children's Books, a division of HarperCollins Publishers, 195 Broadway, New York, NY 10007. www.harpercollinschildrens.com. Watercolor paints and ink were used to prepare the full-color art. The text type is 22-point Bernhard Gothic SG-Extra Heavy. Library of Congress Cataloging-in-Publication Data Henkes, Kevin. Old bear / by Kevin Henkes. p. cm. "Greenwillow Books." Summary: When Old Bear falls asleep for the winter, he has a dream that he is a cub again, enjoying each of the four seasons. ISBN 978-0-06-155205-2 (trade bdg.) ISBN 978-0-06-155206-9 (lib. bdg.) [1. Bears—Fiction. 2. Dreams—Fiction. 3. Seasons—Fiction. 4. Hibernation—Fiction.] I. Title. PZ7.H389Okh 2008 [E]—dc22 2007035965 First Edition 16 17 18 19 20 SCP 10 9

Greenwillow Books  An Imprint of HarperCollinsPublishers

# OLD BEAR

## KEVIN HENKES